W9-BUF-476

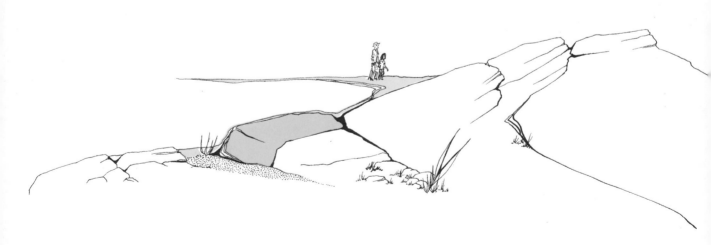

THE OTHER WAY TO LISTEN

BY BYRD BAYLOR AND PETER PARNALL

ALADDIN PAPERBACKS

First Aladdin Paperbacks edition December 1997
Text copyright © 1978 by Byrd Baylor
Illustrations copyright © 1978 by Peter Parnall

Aladdin Paperbacks
An imprint of Simon & Schuster Children's Publishing Division
1230 Avenue of the Americas, New York, NY 10020

All rights reserved, including the right of
reproduction in whole or in part in any form.
Manufactured in China

40 39 38 37 36 35 34 33

The Library of Congress has cataloged the hardcover edition as follows:
Baylor, Byrd.
The other way to listen.
Summary: After hoping and trying, the narrator is finally able to hear
the hills singing.
[1. Nature—Poetry.   2. American poetry]   I. Parnall, Peter.   II. Title.
PS3552.A87807   811'.5'4   78-23430
ISBN 0-684-16017-X

ISBN 0-689-81053-9 (Aladdin pbk.) (ISBN-13: 978-0-689-81053-4)
1222 SCP

For Riki, Jesse, and Zak

I used to know
an old man
who could
walk
by any
cornfield
and hear
the corn
singing.

"Teach me,"
I'd say
when we'd
passed on by.
(I never said
a word
while he was
listening.)

"Just tell me
how
you learned
to hear
that
corn."

And he'd say,
"It takes
a lot of
practice.
You can't
be
in a hurry."

And I'd say,
"I have
the time."

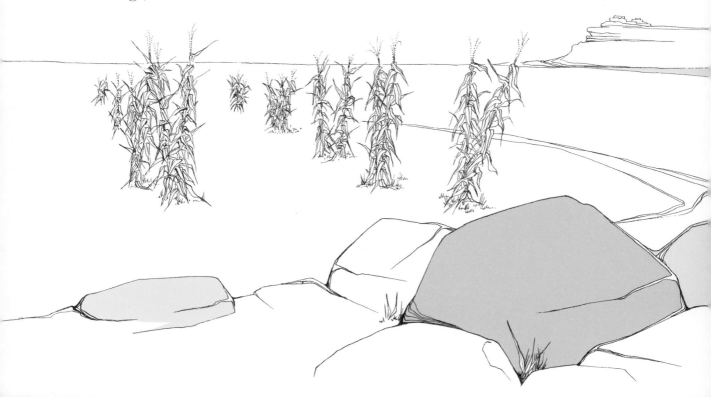

He was so
good
at listening—
once
he heard
wildflower seeds
burst open,
beginning
to grow
underground.

That's hard to do.

He said
he was just
lucky
to have been
by himself
up there
in the canyon
after a rain.

He said
it was the
quietest place
he'd ever been
and he stayed there
long enough to
understand
the quiet.

I said,
"I bet you were
surprised
when you heard
those seeds."

But
he said,
"No,
I wasn't surprised at all.
It seemed like the most
natural
thing
in the world."

He just smiled,
remembering.

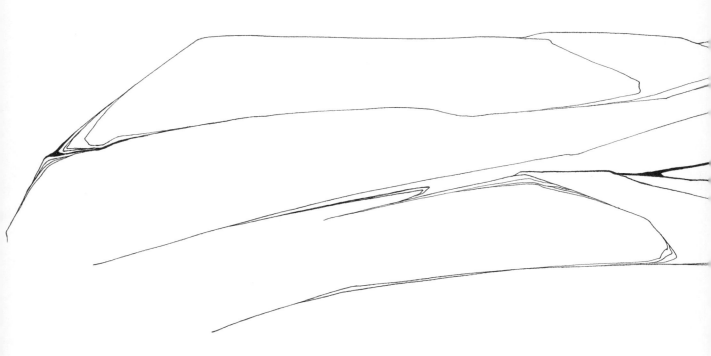

Another time
he heard
a rock
kind of
murmur
good things
to a lizard.

I was there.

We saw the lizard
sunning
on a rock.
Of course,
we stopped.

The old man said,
"I wonder how
that lizard
feels
about the rock it's
sitting on
and how the rock
feels
about the lizard?"

He always
asked himself
hard
questions
that take
awhile
to answer.

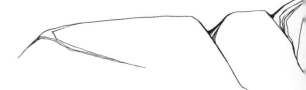

We leaned against
another rock.
A long time
passed,
and then
he said,
"Did you hear that?
They like each other
fine."

I said,
"I didn't hear
a thing.

He said,
"Sometimes
EVERYTHING
BEING RIGHT
makes a kind of
sound.

Like just now.
It wasn't much more
than a
good feeling
that I heard
from that old rock."

"Were you surprised
to hear it?"
I always had
to ask.

He said,
"Not a bit.
It seemed like the most
natural
thing
in the world."

I said,
"I wish
I'd heard it
too."

He said he thought
I might
someday.

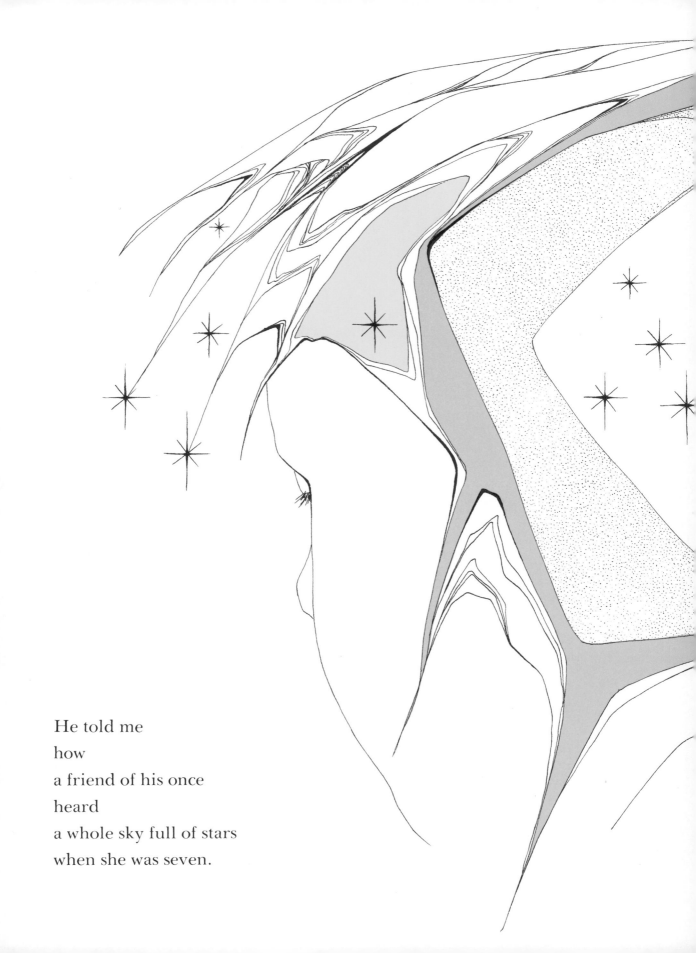

He told me
how
a friend of his once
heard
a whole sky full of stars
when she was seven.

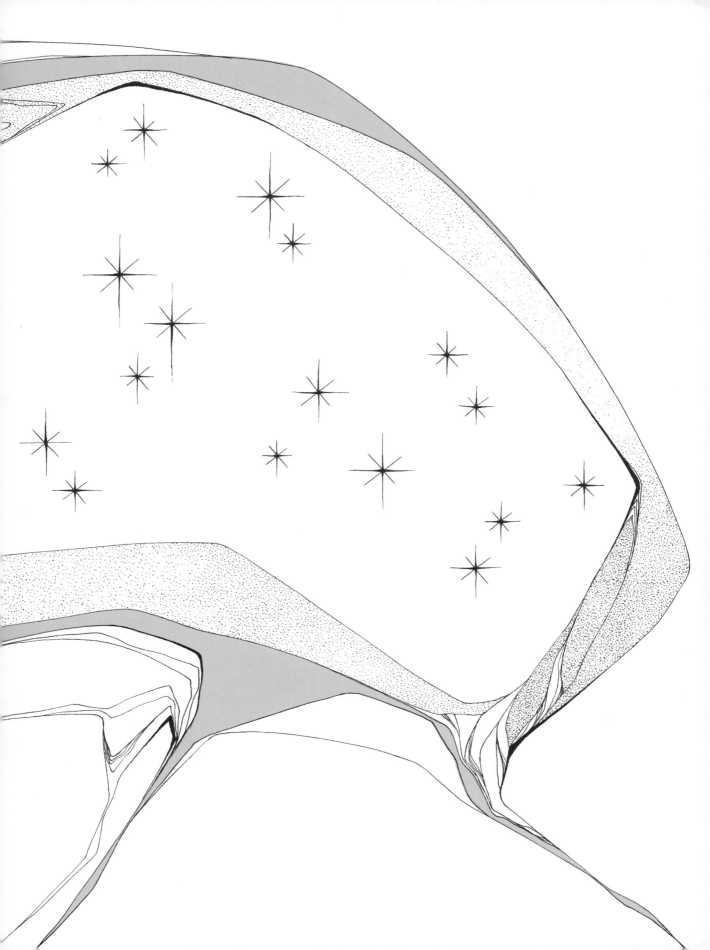

And later on
when she was eighty three
she heard
a cactus
blooming
in the dark.

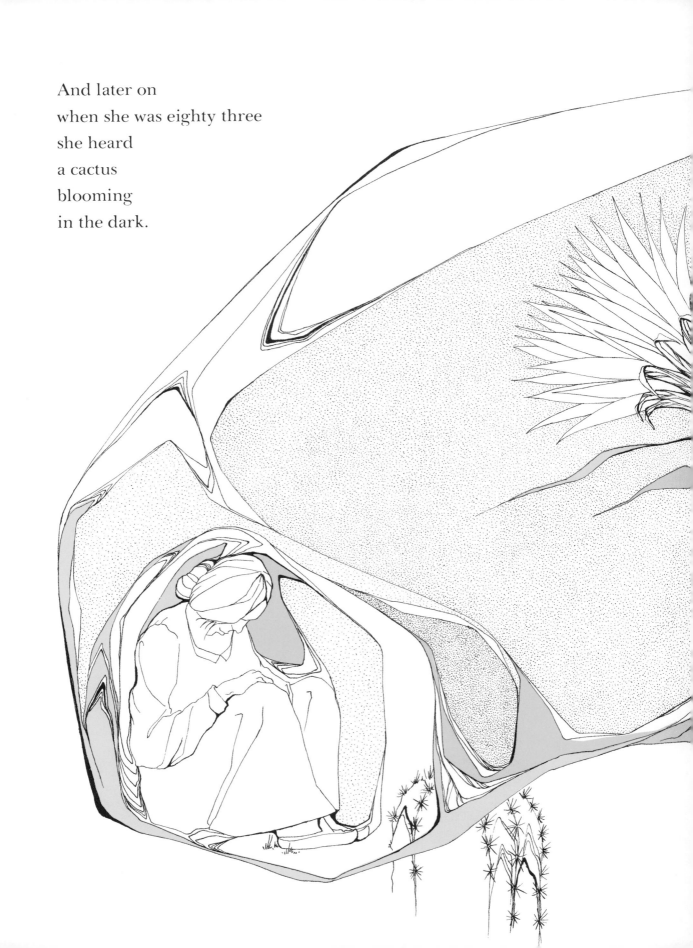

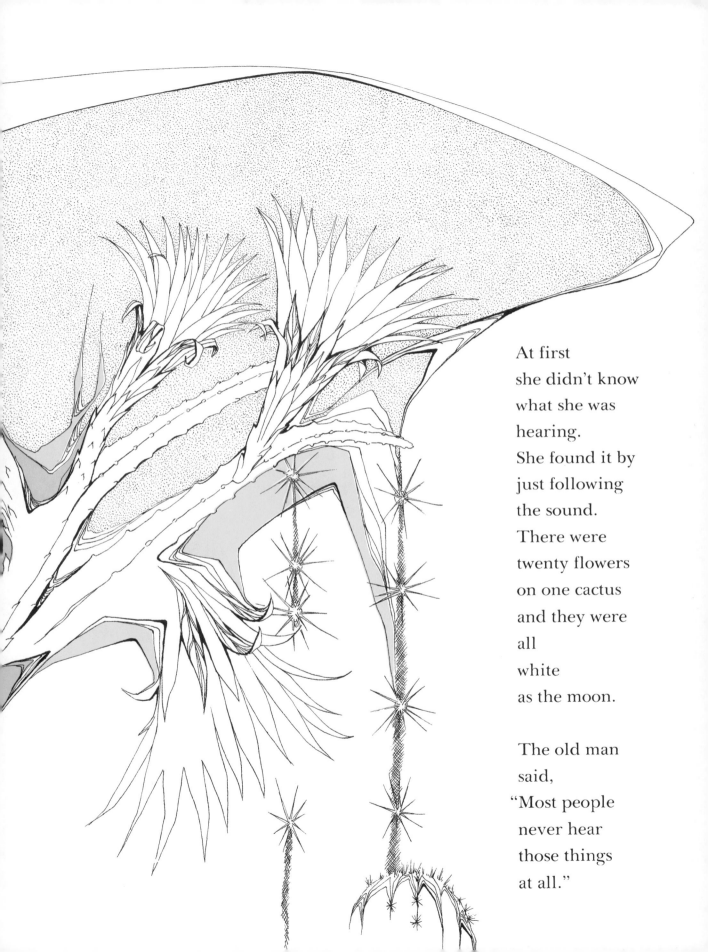

At first
she didn't know
what she was
hearing.
She found it by
just following
the sound.
There were
twenty flowers
on one cactus
and they were
all
white
as the moon.

The old man
said,
"Most people
never hear
those things
at all."

I said,
"I wonder why."

He said,
"They just
 don't take the time
 you need
 for something
 that
 important."

I said,
"I'll take the time.
 But first
 you have to teach me."

"I'd like to
 if I could,"
 he said,
"but the thing is…
 you have to
 learn it
 from
 the hills
 and ants
 and lizards
 and weeds
 and things
 like that.
 They do
 the
 teaching
 around here."

"Just give me
a clue
on
how
to start,"
I said.

And so
he said,
"Do this:
go get to know
one thing
as well
as you can.

It should be
something
small.

Don't start
with a mountain.
Don't start
with the whole
Pacific Ocean.

Start with
one seed pod
or
one dry weed
or
one
horned toad
or
one
handful
of dirt
or
one
sandy wash."

I said,
"I'll take
the sandy wash."

He said
he started
with
one tree.

Every morning
of his life
when he was young
he climbed
a cottonwood
and sat there
listening.

He told me
it was worth
the time.
He said
trees
are very honest
and they don't
care much
for fancy people.
And he said
he doesn't know
of anything
he ever did
as important
as sitting
in that tree.

"Tell me everything
you can,"
I said.

He said,
"Well,
you have to
respect
that tree
or
hill
or whatever it is
you're
with.

Take a horned toad,
for example.
If you think
you're
better
than a horned toad
you'll
never
hear its voice—
even if you
sit there in the sun
forever."

And he said,
"Don't be
ashamed
to learn
from
bugs
or
sand
or anything."

I said,
"I *won't*."

He thought of
one more thing.

"It's good to
walk
with people
but
sometimes
go alone."

"That way,"
he said,
"you can always
stop
and listen
at the right time."

"I'll
remember
everything,"
I said.

And I did.

But
nothing worked.

I thought
there must be
something
wrong
with me
because
I only heard
wind
and quail
and coyotes
and doves—
just things that
anyone
could hear.

I almost
gave up
trying.

Of course
I still
went
walking
in my hills.

In fact,
I used to
sing
to them
a lot.
I thought
that since
they wouldn't
sing
to me,
I'd just
sing to them
instead.

The day
I'm telling you about
now
I was
singing
and the whole song
was this:
HELLO HILLS
HELLO HILLS
HELLO HILLS
HELLO.

That was after
I had been away
five days
and I had
missed
those hills—
five days.

I went out
earlier
than usual.

You know how
everything
looks
new
at sunrise.
Well,
all those hills
were looking
new.

I was
just
walking
where I
always walk
but
that
morning
I kept thinking
HERE I AM!

And
whatever way
I happened
to go
was
always
right.

I climbed
the rocky side,
not the path.
The rocky side
is steeper
but I like it
best,
and anyway
that's where
I found
my three
hawk
feathers.

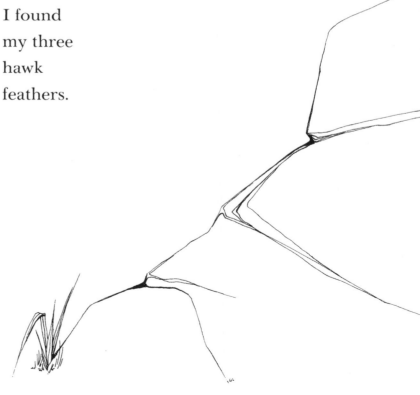

I stood
at the top
where I always stand
looking down.

HELLO HILLS
HELLO HILLS
HELLO HILLS
HELLO.

All I know is

suddenly

I wasn't
the only one
singing.

The hills
were
singing
too.

I stopped.

I didn't move
for
maybe
an hour.

I never
listened
so hard
hard
in my life.

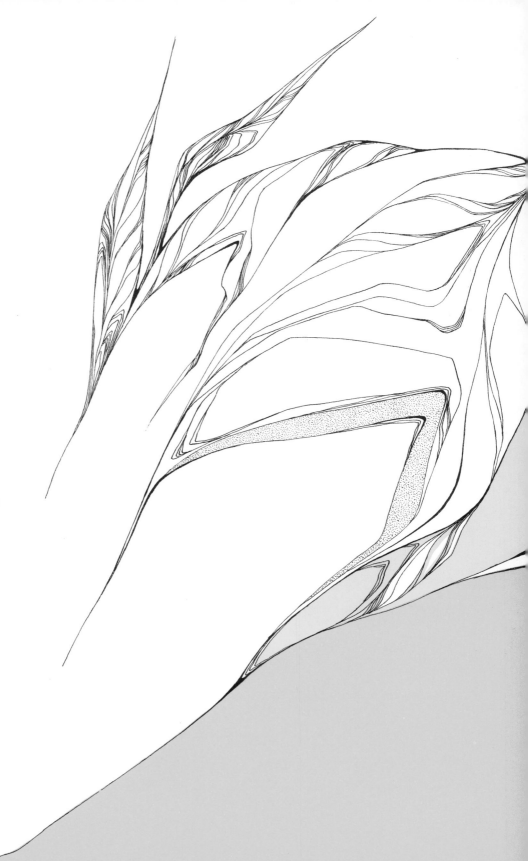

Of course
their kind of singing
isn't loud.

It isn't
any sound
you can explain.

It isn't
made
with words.

You couldn't
write it down.

All I can say
is
it came
straight up
from
those
dark shiny lava rocks
humming.
It moved around
like
wind.

It seemed to be
the oldest
sound
in the world.

All I can say
is
I was
standing
in the middle
of that sound
at seven o'clock
in the morning…

just thinking
HERE I AM!

and thinking
LISTEN!

and not even
being surprised.

It seemed like
the most
natural
thing
in the world.